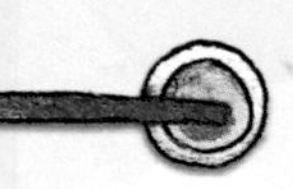

My Firstborn, There's No One Like You

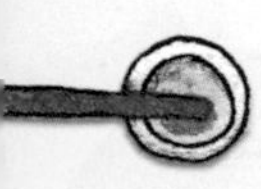

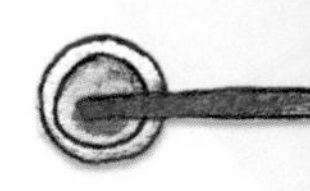

Dear Mama and Papa Bear:

It's all about birth order.

Your firstborn has unique qualities special only to him or her. Did you know that

- twenty-one of the first twenty-three astronauts in space were firstborns and the other two were the only child in their family?
- your CPA, engineer, architect, pilot, and anesthesiologist are probably firstborns?
- by and large, most of our former presidents were either the first child or the first of their sex in their family?

There's no hiding the fact that your firstborn is special. And nothing can compare to the feelings you have for him or her. By now he probably has started to reflect characteristics of being a strong leader. I'd bet that she has shown signs of being conscientious, well organized, and hardworking—all qualities common to a perfectionist firstborn cub. With every passing day, you love him or her even more.

And isn't it amazing how cubs, all from the same den, can be so different? That is why we wrote *My Firstborn, There's No One Like You*. It's a fun way to celebrate your first! We guarantee that no matter what age he or she is—whether all grown up or still a little cub—your firstborn will love it. Give it as a gift or read it together to show him or her just how special he or she really is. Either way, we hope you enjoy it!

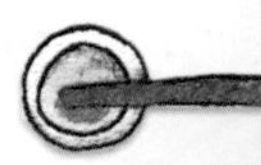

My Firstborn, There's No One Like You

Dr. Kevin Leman
& Kevin Leman II

Illustrated by
Kevin Leman II

Revell
Grand Rapids, Michigan

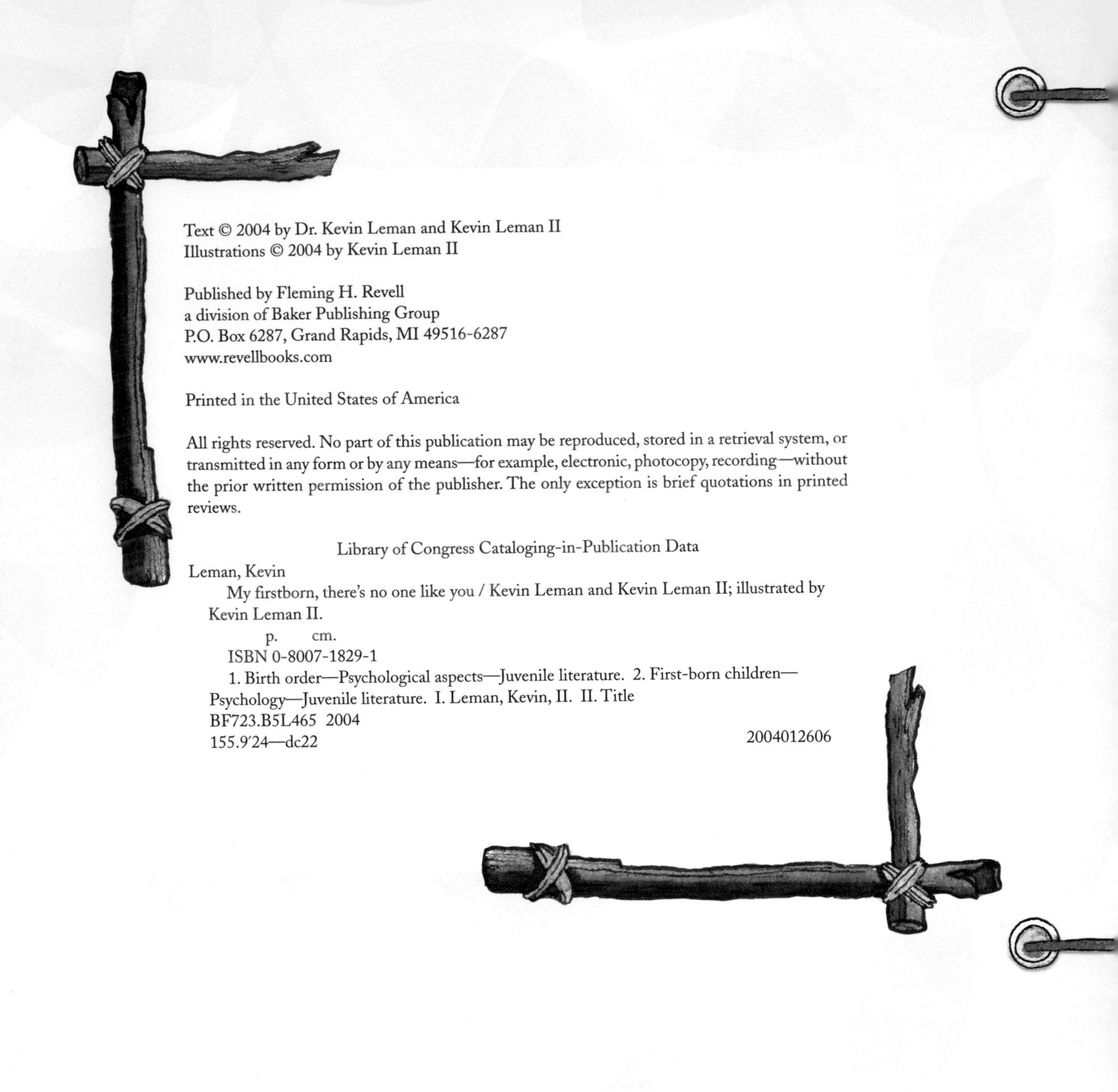

Published by Fleming H. Revell
a division of Baker Publishing Group
P.O. Box 6287, Grand Rapids, MI 49516-6287
www.revellbooks.com

Printed in the United States of America

Library of Congress Cataloging-in-Publication Data

Leman, Kevin
My firstborn, there's no one like you / Kevin Leman and Kevin Leman II; illustrated by Kevin Leman II.
p. cm.
ISBN 0-8007-1829-1
1. Birth order—Psychological aspects—Juvenile literature. 2. First-born children—Psychology—Juvenile literature. I. Leman, Kevin, II. II. Title
BF723.B5L465 2004
155.9′24—dc22 2004012606

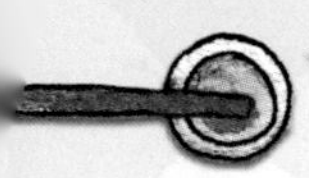

To my mom and dad . . . I love you the best.

—Kevin Leman II

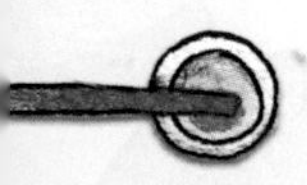

Three little cubs come out of the same den, and, oh my, are they different!

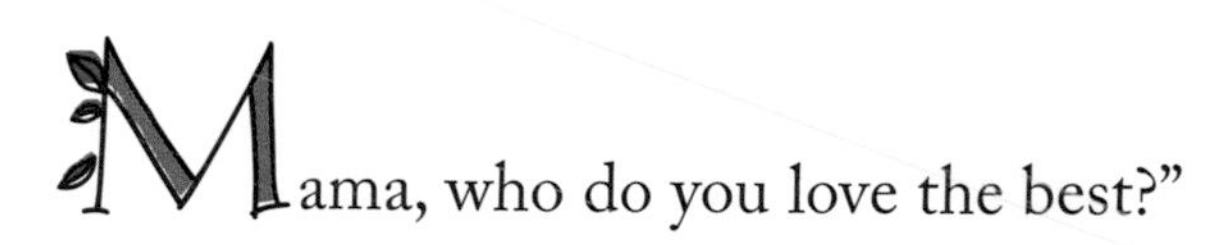

Mama, who do you love the best?”

“Is that what you cubs were arguing about in there?”

“Maybe.”

“Well, that’s a very tricky question for a mama bear to answer.” Mama sat down in her favorite storytelling chair and reached over to pick up a photo album. “Let’s see . . .”

The day you were born!

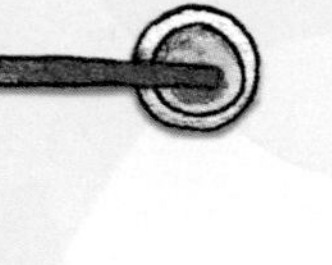

Mama Bear pulled her firstborn cub onto her lap. "I still remember the day you were born. I was so happy when the nurse put you into my arms, I cried. You were our precious gift from God. I leaned down and nuzzled your tiny face and whispered, 'I love you.' And Papa was so proud, I thought he'd burst! He took two hours of video that day and another two hours the day we brought you home!"

"How long are the videos of the other cubs?"

"Not *that* long. And you kept sticking your face into most of them!" Mama Bear smiled as she opened the photo album. "This book—oh my, it's filled with adorable pictures of you. Your baby sister doesn't even have a photo album of her own."

"Does that mean you love me the best, Mama?"

"Well, let's see . . ."

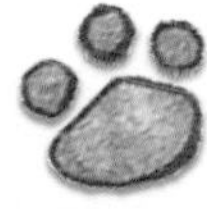 

Everything was new for you, because you were our first cub. Grandma and Grandpa pitched in to help create the perfect bedroom for you with everything in its place. Everything was new—new crib, new changing table, new diaper bag." Mama Bear laughed. "Papa baby-proofed every room of the den. He blocked the stairs so you wouldn't tumble down, and he covered up anything that could hurt you. I read a whole stack of books just to learn how to raise you."

"Did you do all that with the other cubs?"

Mama Bear shook her head. "No, I guess we didn't."

Firstborn Cub cast a quick glance at the cubs playing in the next room and whispered, "So does that mean you love me the best?"

"Well, let's see . . ."

Firstborn Cub's bedroom—everything is perfect!

Some
before-school
excitement!

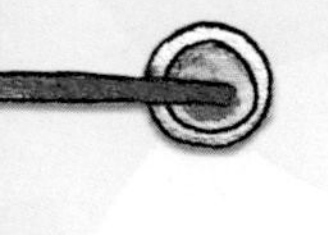

"The truth is," Mama Bear said as she turned the page, "sometimes you were downright persnickety! Everything had to be just the way you wanted it. When you were a baby cub, you had to be rocked a certain way. Then you had to brush your teeth with a green toothbrush, but you would drink only from a blue cup. At bedtime, you had to have the door opened exactly halfway, and when we tucked you in, the quilt had to be over your shoulders but not touching your chin."

Firstborn Cub giggled. "That was silly."

Mama Bear laughed. "And when you ate spaghetti, the sauce couldn't touch the noodles. You made me take the crusts off your honey and peanut butter sandwiches. You were unhappy if your socks weren't on straight or a shirt tag was rubbing your neck. You were quite a bit of work, as I recall."

"Does that mean you love the other cubs the best?"

"Well, let's see . . ."

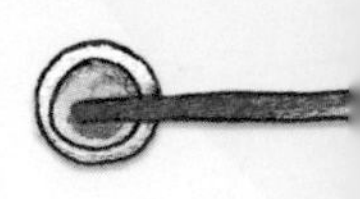

Your first day of school!

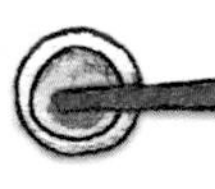

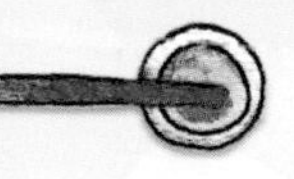

"I don't think I've ever done anything as hard as dropping you off at school the first day," Mama Bear said. "I wasn't ready to watch you go, but you marched into the classroom like a brave soldier. That's when I realized my little firstborn wasn't so little anymore."

Firstborn Cub nodded. "I remember that day."

"I'm sure you do! You immediately liked your teacher and found a playmate. Right away you discovered books would be some of your closest friends. And back home, even though your brother and sister were still there with me, the den seemed extra empty that day. I kept watching the clock. I could hardly wait until you came home."

"You missed me even though the other cubs were home? That must mean you love me the best!"

"Well, let's see . . ."

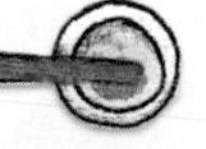

Cubs
win in extra
innings!

"It was always nice having you around," Mama Bear admitted. "I loved how you helped with your brother and sister. You showed them how to do all sorts of things. You've always been a helper and a leader. I honestly don't know how I could have raised the other cubs without you. They're so lucky to have you. I'm sure they'll always look to you during sticky situations."

"That's *them*, Mama, but what about *you*? Do you love me the best?"

"Well, let's see . . ."

Mama Bear flipped a page of the photo album and began to laugh.

"What's so funny?"

"You always liked to give your sister a hard time. Since the day we brought her home, you weren't so sure she should stay," Mama Bear said. "You spent hours watching her sleep. Then you came to me at dinner and said, 'Mama, maybe Gramma Bear can take her.'" Mama Bear laughed again. "You wanted to give her away!"

Firstborn Cub started to fidget. "So do you love her the best?"

"Well, let's see . . ."

Oh, the things you put your sister through!

Sitting with the grown-ups
at Thanksgiving.

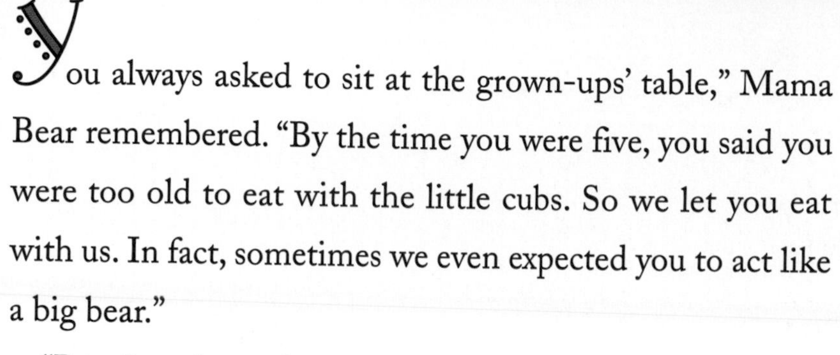

You always asked to sit at the grown-ups' table," Mama Bear remembered. "By the time you were five, you said you were too old to eat with the little cubs. So we let you eat with us. In fact, sometimes we even expected you to act like a big bear."

"But the other cubs never ate at the grown-ups' table, did they, Mama?"

"No, honey, they didn't."

"So does that mean you've always loved me the best?"

"Well, let's see . . ."

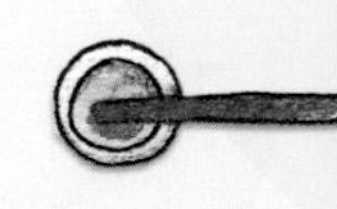

You sure kept things interesting," Mama Bear said. "Oh, the plays you put on for us! You were always the director *and* played the leading role. Somehow your sister always wound up playing the ugly stepsister, and your brother played a dog!"

"He made a *good* dog."

Mama Bear smiled. "And you liked organizing contests for singing, dancing, coloring—whatever you were good at."

"I always won, didn't I, Mama?"

"Yes, I guess you did. But that's not all I love about you."

"You mean there's more?"

"Well, let's see . . ."

The director and star
of our family play.

You made sure no one sneaked a peek!

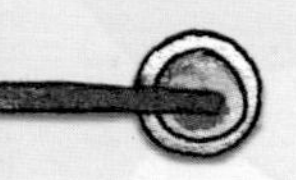

"I love the way you helped create so many traditions for our family," Mama Bear said. "Do you remember how you started the only-one-gift-at-a-time rule at Christmas?"

Firstborn Cub nodded eagerly. "And we still do that!"

"Yes, and you started the Family Christmas Show, the Honey Hoedown, the Forest Find, and the Summer Splish 'n' Splash."

"What else do you love about me?"

"Well, let's see . . ."

Even when you were a little cub, you were always full of ideas!" Mama Bear said. "Your powerful little mind never took a break. You wanted to know how everything worked. And the questions—oh my—they never stopped! You asked things like, 'Do bunnies go to heaven?' or 'If God made lightning bugs, did he make thunder bugs too?' I remember the time your papa came home after your first Forest Find. He was so tired from all those questions. He couldn't even answer them all. But here is one answer I think you'll like . . ."

You and Papa go
on a Forest Find!

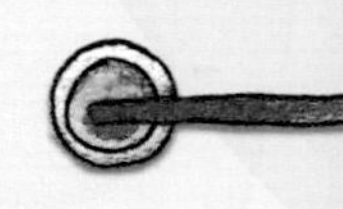

Mama Bear tells a special secret.

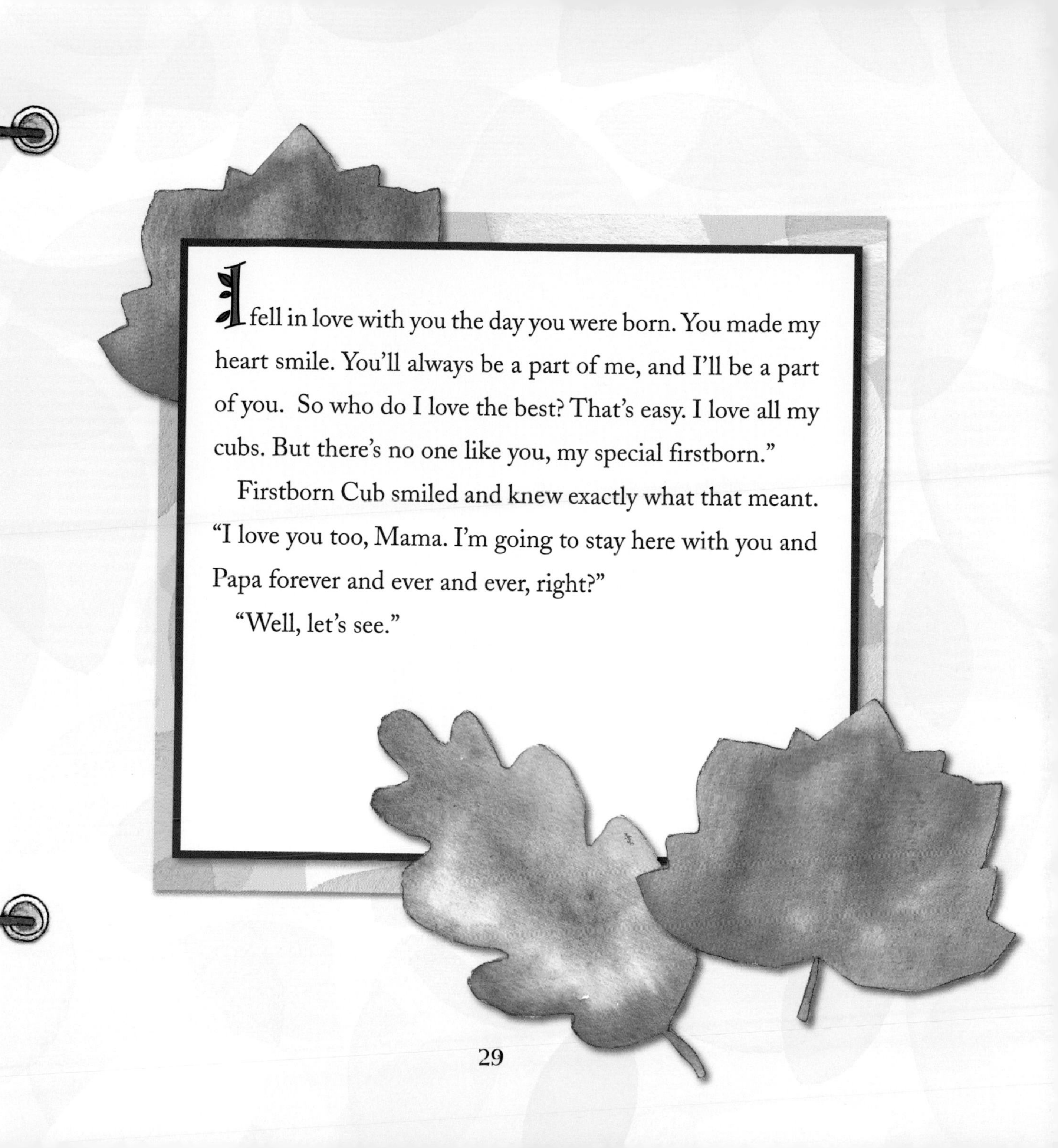

I fell in love with you the day you were born. You made my heart smile. You'll always be a part of me, and I'll be a part of you. So who do I love the best? That's easy. I love all my cubs. But there's no one like you, my special firstborn."

Firstborn Cub smiled and knew exactly what that meant. "I love you too, Mama. I'm going to stay here with you and Papa forever and ever and ever, right?"

"Well, let's see."

Don't let your middle and youngest children miss out on all the fun!

Middle Cub, look at this! There are hardly any pictures of us!

That's because we each have our own books coming in 2005!

Dr. Kevin Leman & Kevin Leman II
My Middle Child, There's No One Like You

Dr. Kevin Leman & Kevin Leman II
My Youngest, There's No One Like You
Illustrated by Kevin Leman II

Dr. Kevin Leman & Kevin Leman II
My Firstborn, There's No One Like You

Coming soon

My Middle Child, There's No One Like You	Spring 2005
My Youngest, There's No One Like You	Spring 2005

Years later Mama Bear and her firstborn cub enjoy a special moment. And, by the way, Firstborn Cub did leave home!